I READ-N-RHYME

A CRABTREE SEEDLINGS BOOK

Captain Blarney

The Pirates' Battle for Bedtime

Sebastian Smith

CRABTREE
PUBLISHING COMPANY
WWW.CRABTREEBOOKS.COM

On a tiring, long voyage
across the seas of life,
sailed a captain so rough,
so tumble, and sharp as a knife.

His name was Blarney,
but his men called him Big,
even though he was small
and had one wooden leg.

The work was hard,
and the days were long.

The pirates needed sleep,
to make them strong.

Seven days of pillage,
seven nights of plunder.
They battled ships on the surface,
but feared the creatures
down under.

Big ordered his mates to hoist the sail.

"It's time to head home. But watch out for the stay-awake whale!"

The mate in the crow's nest had spotted the whale.
The men were instructed to tie up its tail.

They made their way onward
and the wind it did howl.
The slimy no-sleep squid
slithered up the ship's bow.

The captain ordered his men to fire a cannon ball.

"Knock that terrible creature overboard!"

Onward they went,
getting closer to their beds,
knowing they could finally
lay down their sleepy heads.

But the fight wasn't over.
Their strength would be tested.

From the water came old pirates—
the bones of the unrested.

With swords in their hands
and fear in their eyes,
the captain yelled "**GET**
'EM" and they fought for
their lives.

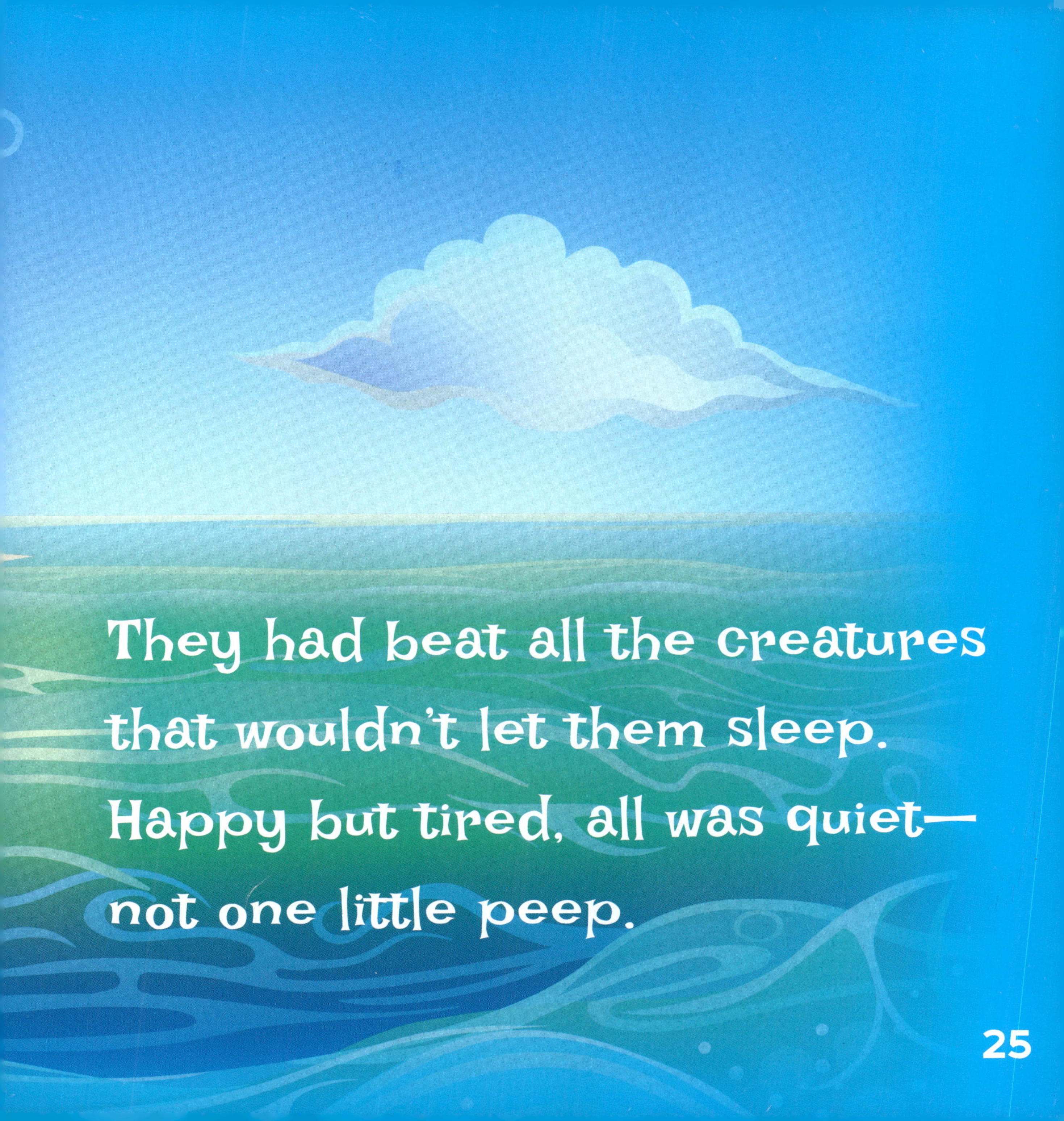

They had beat all the creatures
that wouldn't let them sleep.
Happy but tired, all was quiet—
not one little peep.

Three cheers for Big,
a captain true and strong.
He'd got them home safe,
and in bed where they belonged.

"Good night, maties!
Aaaarrrrgggghhhh!"

School-to-Home Support for Caregivers and Teachers

Crabtree Seedlings books help children grow by letting them practice reading. Here are a few guiding questions to help the reader build his or her comprehension skills. Possible answers are included.

Before Reading

- **What do I think this book is about?** I think this book is a story about pirates who want to go to sleep.
- **What do I want to learn about this topic?** I want to learn the kinds of battles fought by the pirates in the story. Do they battle a squid like the one on the cover?

During Reading

- **I wonder why…** I wonder why Captain Blarney is called Big, even though he looks small.
- **What have I learned so far?** I learned that the pirates in the story battled other pirate ships, creatures under the water, and pirate skeletons!

After Reading

- **What details did I learn about this topic?** I learned that pirates face many different challenges and work hard to overcome them.
- **Write down unfamiliar words and ask questions to help understand their meaning.** I see the word ***voyage*** on page 2. The words "tiring" and "long" describe voyage. Is it a type of journey? I also wonder about the word ***hoist*** on page 10. What does it mean?

Library and Archives Canada Cataloguing in Publication

Title: Captain Blarney : the pirates' battle for bedtime / Sebastian Smith.
Names: Smith, Sebastian, 1996- author.
Description: Series statement: I read-n-rhyme | "A Crabtree seedlings book". | Previously published in electronic format by Blue Door Education in 2020.
Identifiers: Canadiana 20200379003 | ISBN 9781427129192 (hardcover) | ISBN 9781427129307 (softcover)
Classification: LCC PZ7.1.S65 Ca 2021 | DDC j813/.6—dc23

Library of Congress Cataloging-in-Publication Data

Names: Smith, Sebastian, 1996- author.
Title: Captain Blarney : the pirates' battle for bedtime / Sebastian Smith.
Description: New York, NY : Crabtree Publishing, 2021. | Series: Crabtree seedlings. I read-n-rhyme
Identifiers: LCCN 2020048921 | ISBN 9781427129192 (hardcover) | ISBN 9781427129307 (paperback)
Subjects: LCSH: Readers (Primary) | Pirates--Juvenile fiction.
Classification: LCC PE1119.2 .S55 2021 | DDC 428.6/2--dc23
LC record available at https://lccn.loc.gov/2020048921

Crabtree Publishing Company
www.crabtreebooks.com 1–800–387–7650

Author: Sebastian Smith
Production coordinator and Prepress technician: Tammy McGarr
Print coordinator: Katherine Berti

e-book ISBN 978-1-952398-04-9

Print book version produced jointly with Blue Door Education in 2021

Printed in the U.S.A./012021/CG20201102

Illustrations: Cover: background illustration including ship © Vladislav Kudoyarov, pirate in the crow's nest © Meilun, squid © escova, Big aka Captain Blarney throughout book © Armation; pages 2-3, 6-7 © Vladislav Kudoyarov; pages 4-5 © cannon; pages 8-9 and 10-11 ocean © revoltan, sea creatures © escobar; pages 12-13 ocean and ship © Vladislav Kudoyarov, pirate in the crow's nest © Meilun, pages 14-15 ocean and ship © Vladislav Kudoyarov, squid © escova; pages 16-17 ship deuce © cannon, actual cannon and cannonball © Maciej Es; pages 18-19 © Vladislav Kudoyarov; pages 20-21 ship deuce © cannon, skeletons © Klara Viskova; pages 24-25 © leric; pages 26-27 © dip; back cover © Vladislav Kudoyarov, Big © Armation All illustrations from Shutterstock.com

Published in Canada
Crabtree Publishing
616 Welland Ave.
St. Catharines, Ontario
L2M 5V6

Published in the United States
Crabtree Publishing
347 Fifth Ave.
Suite 1402-145
New York, NY 10016

Published in the United Kingdom
Crabtree Publishing
Maritime House
Basin Road North, Hove
BN41 1WR

Published in Australia
Crabtree Publishing
Unit 3 – 5 Currumbin Court
Capalaba
QLD 4157